Un gros bisou por mon
bon ami Michael. Attention de
Monsieur Gravité!

Avec de bons souvenirs,

Madame

This book is a gift to you so that you will always remember Madame
Crabtree. She loved teaching you and being a part of your life.

The inscription inside your book reads:
A big kiss for my good friend _____
Be careful of Mister Gravity
With many fond memories
                    Madame

To our niece, beloved Amy Lynn, who lived life on the edge of gravity.
To all adventurous and cautious children: God loves you all.

- Marjorie Kerr Crabtree

www.mascotbooks.com

For more information, please contact:
Mascot Books
560 Herndon Parkway #120
Herndon, VA 20170
info@mascotbooks.com

Library of Congress Control Number: 2012952891

CPSIA Code: PRT0213A
ISBN-10: 1620861879
ISBN-13: 9781620861875

Printed in the United States

Amy Lynn
On the Edge of Gravity

Marjorie Kerr Crabtree

Illustrated by
Linda Mathesius

When Amy Lynn was almost five, she went to visit her Aunt Marjorie and Uncle Keith. She loved running around their house, jumping from the third step of the basement stairs, and balancing as she skipped along the garden's stone wall.

One morning for breakfast, Aunt Marjorie was making a strawberry smoothie for her niece. On the other side of the kitchen, Amy was intent on twirling as fast as she could on a stool. The blender was loudly swirling strawberries, a banana, and milk. Amy was quietly swirling herself around and around on the stool. In a flash, Amy was yelling louder than the blender's motor. Now the blender was quiet, and Aunt Marjorie ran over to see her niece crying and holding her knee, punctured by a Lego block left on the ground. Due to an earlier scrape or two, the Band-Aid box and the antibiotic ointment were already on the counter. Aunt Marjorie opened the box to find only one Band-Aid left.

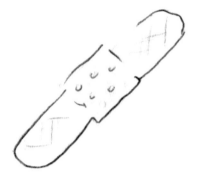

"Amy, this is my last Band-Aid." Aunt Marjorie paused and looked up at the ceiling. "I'm wondering...I'm wondering..."

"What are you wondering?" asked Amy with curiosity.

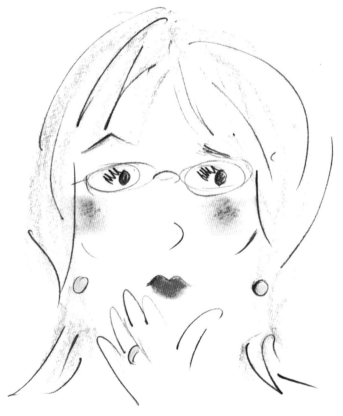

Aunt Marjorie answered slowly, "I'm wondering if there is a way to help you avoid all these scrapes." She stood there with one eyebrow up and one hand over her mouth, thoughtful-like. Finally, she asked, "Has anybody ever talked to you about Mr. Gravity?"

Amy looked up from her skinned knee, wiped her eyes, and said, "I don't know any Mr. Grabity."

Aunt Marjorie said slowly, "Gravity, Mr. Gravity, or Mr. G for short. He has only one rule. Here it is: stay on the ground, or he will bring you down. And he may bring you down hard."

"Well, why does he do that?" asked Amy. "That sounds pretty mean. I don't think I like Mr. Grabity."

"Well, he's not all bad. Why if it weren't for him, your food wouldn't stay on your plate. Think about brushing your teeth and how the water and toothpaste would go swirling out into the air. And your mom wouldn't like that at all, would she? And if you wore your pretty pink poodle skirt, how embarrassing! It just would not stay down."

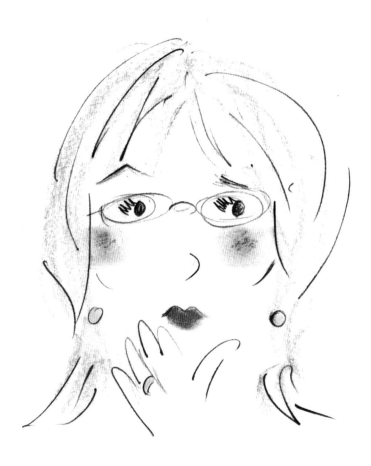

Amy giggled, "And if I jumped, I could go all the way to the moon. That would be fun!" Amy bent her knee to jump, but stopped and winced in pain. That new scrape hurt. Instead, she looked worried and asked, "You mean I can't jump anymore 'cause Mr. Grabity is going to grab me and throw me to the ground hard?"

Aunt Marjorie hugged Amy and smiled, "Sure you can jump, but think about how and where you want to land. Think before you jump." Aunt Marjorie paused with one eyebrow up and one hand over her mouth, thoughtful-like. "You know, there is one way to escape Mr. Gravity's grip. Hitch a ride on a big rocket ship with huge, powerful engines. Only thing is, that costs a lot of money. How much money do you have?"

Amy dug into the pockets of her shorts, and pulled out a candy wrapper, a plastic ring, one quarter, and two pennies. Amy offered up the change to her aunt and asked hopefully, "Is this enough?"

Aunt Marjorie shook her head 'no' and added, "Well, I guess you're stuck here on planet Earth with Mr. Gravity."

Now it was Amy Lynn's turn to think. One eyebrow up and one small hand over her mouth, copying her aunt. "But I want to know something. Is Mr. Grabity a boy or a girl?"

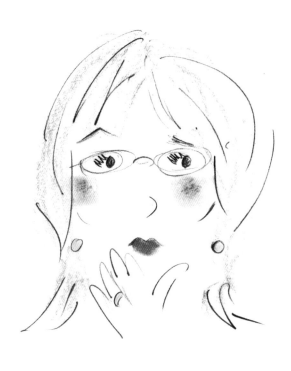

Now it was Aunt Marjorie's turn to think. One eyebrow up, one hand over her mouth, thoughtful-like. Aunt Marjorie started out slowly, "Well, he's actually a force. The ground, the Earth, is kind of like a giant magnet and gravity is the thing that pulls everything down." Aunt Marjorie, who was a teacher, looked pleased with her answer, and she began to repeat, as teachers do, "Now, Amy, remember gravity always..."

Amy looked impatient and insisted, "So, is Mr. Grabity a boy or a girl?"

Aunt Marjorie smiled, "He's a boy, Amy."

"Thought so," said Amy. That's all she needed to know.

That night after dinner, Uncle Keith asked if anybody felt like having some ice cream. "Yes, yes, yes!" screamed Amy. She almost started to jump up and down in her excitement for ice cream, but she remembered her knee. Instead, she twirled. "Yes! Of course!"

Aunt Marjorie started the song, "I scream, you scream, we all scream for ice cream."

Amy continued the chant all the way to the ice cream parlor. Once there, Uncle Keith ordered one large scoop of mint chocolate chip in a waffle cone. Aunt Marjorie ordered one small scoop of double chocolate and one small scoop of raspberry sorbet in a cup. Amy ordered one large scoop of strawberry with sprinkles in a waffle cone.

As the three sat on a bench and licked their sweet treats, they watched a little squirrel scurrying around. It was a warm, beautiful summer evening. Amy swung her legs as she licked her big pink scoop with her little pink tongue. *Drip, drip, drip. Lick, lick, lick.* Aunt Marjorie looked over just as that scoop started to tilt, and before she could catch that scoop, a pink mushy mess lay on the ground. Amy held an empty cone, and her eyes welled up with tears. Mr. Gravity had done it again.

Uncle Keith and Aunt Marjorie looked at each other, each with one eyebrow up, asking the same question without saying a word. The decision was made in a moment. No, this time, Mr. G was not going to win.

So the three got back in line. "One large scoop of strawberry, please, with sprinkles, in a cup, with a waffle cone on top," ordered Uncle Keith. Amy rubbed her once teary eyes with her sticky hands. One happy little girl grinned as she dug into her new pink treat, this time with a spoon. Mr. Gravity did land some drops of ice cream on Amy's white top and pink shorts, but Amy's spoon delivered most of the strawberry delight to her eager tongue.

Aunt Marjorie laughed as she looked at her very contented niece. "Amy, you are a sight. Next stop: the bathtub."

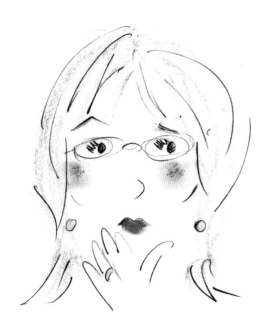

Amy was happy to jump in the tub and dump in a generous amount of bubble bath. The bubbles grew and grew, and some even floated in the air. Would Mr. G pull them down, too? When Amy went to sit down, some bubbly water touched her tender knee. She whimpered. The Band-Aid from earlier in the day was hanging off the cut. Tonight, Amy would not be whipping up a bubble storm. There would be no sunken plastic boats and no large puddles on the bathroom floor. She could only sit with her one injured knee sticking up above the foamy water. So, Aunt Marjorie gently washed away the day's dirt. Then she helped her little patient carefully step out of the tub.

Amy was ready to be done with the stinging bathwater. She knew that story time was next. Amy snuggled into her PJ's, her favorite PJ's, the ones with the parade of black poodles marching across a pink field. They each wore a pink bow on their curly heads, as though they had all just left the dog groomer. Half the poodles paraded to the right; the other half paraded to the left. Amy took her spot in the big brown chair in the pale blue guest room. Aunt Marjorie and Uncle Keith loved this part of the bedtime ritual, and they took turns reading to their niece. The whole time, Amy's favorite plush, pink poodle, Hazelnut, listened too. This treasured toy was held in Amy's arms so the poodle could see the pictures too.

After several books, Amy's eyelids were starting to droop. "I'm not sleepy," she mumbled as she struggled to stay awake. Hazelnut never got sleepy. However, Amy did not protest when Uncle Keith lifted her into the guest bed and tucked her sweet pink poodle into bed with her. Aunt Marjorie bent down and kissed her cheek. Amy whispered, "Goodnight, Aunt Marjorie. Goodnight, Uncle Keith. Goodnight, Hazelnut. Goodnight, Mr. Grabity."

Aunt Marjorie and Uncle Keith tiptoed downstairs. They turned to each other and smiled. Amy had made it through the whole evening without any new bruises or any need for more Band-Aids.

Aunt Marjorie looked thoughtful. One eyebrow up, one hand over her mouth. "I'm thinking. I'm thinking, Keith."

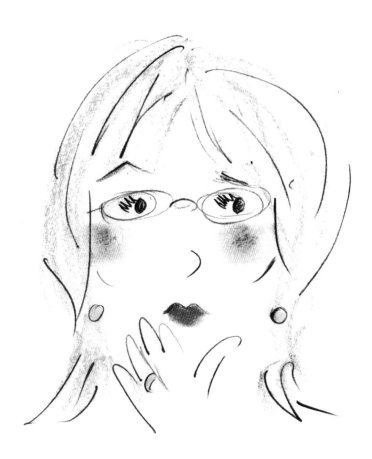

"Yes? Are you thinking about another bowl of ice cream?" suggested Uncle Keith.

"No." Aunt Marjorie was in teacher mode. "My kindergartners learn a lot through songs and poems. Maybe I could write a rhyme to help Amy remember Mr. Gravity." She got out some paper and pen and scribbled some notes. This is what it said:

"God has poured out His love into our hearts."
ROMANS 5:5 NIV

Let me tell you about a girl
Who liked to twirl & swirl

Sunshine on her fun fair face
Smile with an empty space.

After an encounter
With the kitchen counter.

"No, that's not it," murmured Aunt Marjorie. She picked up her pen and started again. Uncle Keith read over Aunt Marjorie's shoulder. Uncle Keith looked thoughtful and scribbled on his own scrap of paper:

Bouncing down the stairs
Bouncing stair to stair
Bounding chair to chair
Catch me catch me if you can
~~I'm way faster than~~
I'm faster than even Superman!

Aunt Marjorie laughed. Over the next few days, Aunt Marjorie and Uncle Keith traded rhymes. Aunt Marjorie wrote:

Amy Lynn, almost 5
Fearless, freckled, fast
She gives hugs and laughs
and ~~heart~~ ♡ attacks
To all the adults around.

Uncle Keith, who loved reading about space exploration and rocket ships, wrote:

Amy standing on a chair
Laun~~ching~~^{ed} herself into the air
Like an astronaut into space
Excitement spread all over her face
~~Careful, careful,~~ you could ~~slip~~
Watch out, Watch out ~~trip~~
flip
Then Mr. Gravity, he will grip
So careful, careful, hear this rule
They don't teach you this in school
Mr Gravity is all around
~~So keep your feet flat on the~~
ground
Ready to bring you back to
the ground

One night, after Amy had been put to bed, Aunt Marjorie was working on one more poem about her niece's battle with gravity. Aunt Marjorie jumped when she heard Amy from around the corner, "Hey, what are you doing?"

Aunt Marjorie did not answer the question. She had her own question. "Aren't you supposed to be in bed?"

"What are you writing?" persisted Amy.

This time, Aunt Marjorie decided to answer. "Uncle Keith and I are trying to write something to help you remember to be safe. Would you like to hear what we wrote?" Amy listened as her aunt read:

Ice cream, cotton candy and all things sweet
A bag of jolly ranchers, but how to reach?
On a stool, wobble, wobble
Careful, or hobble, hobble
Watch out, Amy Lynn
You are cruisin for a bruisin'
One stretch, one step more
Gravity will have you on the floor

Aunt Marjorie held Amy and gave her one of those long, wonderful hugs she loved to give. Then she said, "You are our very special niece, and we don't want you to get hurt."

Amy looked thoughtful with one small hand over her mouth and whispered, "Do you think Mr. Grabity is listening?"

"Well, that I don't know, Amy. You can ponder that question while you're falling asleep." Now Aunt Marjorie looked like a teacher. "No more delays. Up to bed."

The next morning, after two weeks of visits to the zoo, museums, and playgrounds galore, the day had come for Amy to return to her family. Amy's dad had come to take her home to Illinois. "Come on in, Warren," welcomed Aunt Marjorie. Amy jumped, of course, into her dad's arms. After lunch, Aunt Marjorie and Uncle Keith stood in the driveway and waved to a freckled face, framed with golden hair. That face looked back and grinned from the back seat. Right beside that freckled face, a pink poodle stared out the window and waved a paw too.

Over the years, Amy came to visit her Ohio aunt and uncle several times and they, in turn, went to Illinois to see Amy and her family. And every time they saw Amy, they could not help but say, "Wow, you sure have gotten taller." Then came the visit where they had to say, "Wow, you sure have gotten pretty. You look all grown-up." Along came a young man who thought the same thing. Now Josh and Amy are husband and wife, and they have their own little boy who is climbing and jumping.

One day, all grown-up, Amy called her aunt and uncle to share stories about her two-year-old son. She was very proud of Joshua, but she was also worried and tired from trying to keep him safe from accidents. When Aunt Marjorie found out that little Joshua was just like his daring mother had been, she wanted to help. As soon as she hung up the phone, she started looking for those scraps of paper with rhymes that she and Uncle Keith had written for five-year-old Amy. Finally, she found them in the bottom of a drawer and dumped them out in front of Uncle Keith, who picked up a scrap and read:

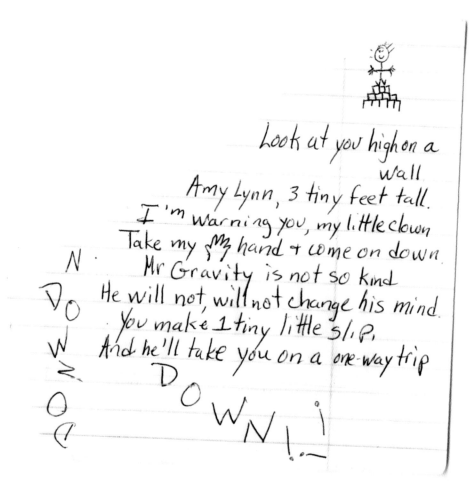

Look at you high on a wall.
Amy Lynn, 3 tiny feet tall.
I'm warning you, my little clown
Take my hand + come on down.
Mr Gravity is not so kind
He will not, will not change his mind.
You make 1 tiny little slip,
And he'll take you on a one-way trip
DOWN!

Another poem was written on a drugstore receipt for Band-Aids. It read:

JOE'S PHARMACY

4610 Main St. Hilliard, OH 43026

Ph: 777-1988

1 BNDAID PL STR 60CT	3.59T
1 NEILMD SINUS 100S	9.99T

2 ITEMS

SUBTOTAL	13.58
OH 6.75% TAX	.92
TOTAL	14.50
CHANGE	0.00

Returns with receipt.

****

Thank you.

****

~~Open Up the garden~~ —
Open wide the garden gates
Here comes Amy on roller skates,
Haven't you seen the TV ads;
Wear your helmet & knee pads!!

It was time to polish those lines up and warn little Joshua. Maybe if he knew about Mr. Grabity early on, he would not need so many bandages. Maybe he wouldn't have to go to the dentist because he broke his teeth from an encounter with the kitchen counter. "Keep it short and to the point," urged Uncle Keith.

"How's this?"

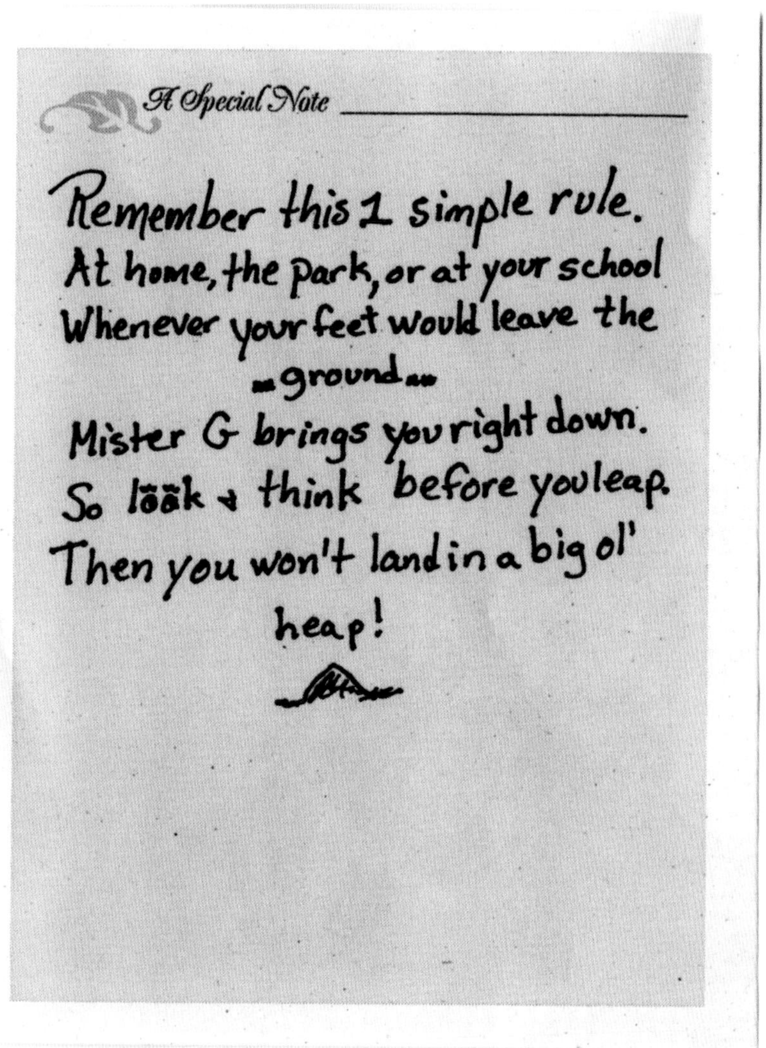

A Special Note _____

Remember this 1 simple rule.
At home, the park, or at your school
Whenever your feet would leave the
ground...
Mister G brings you right down.
So look & think before you leap.
Then you won't land in a big ol'
heap!

"That will do," smiled Uncle Keith.

The End

About the Author

The real Aunt Marjorie is married to the real Uncle Keith. They have two children, Elisabeth and Stephen. They were born a few years after Amy's two week stay with her aunt and uncle. Elisabeth and Stephen benefited from the lessons on Mr. Gravity, originally taught to their cousin, Amy. Marjorie has taught French in high schools in Maryland, Ohio, and Korea. For the last sixteen years, she has taught French to preschoolers and kindergartners at Dublin Montessori Academy. There, she learned that songs, poems, and imagination help teach French, just as they taught Amy about gravity.